To my editor, Joan Powers, for helping me
make everything Better! Better!

First published 2018 by Walker Books Ltd, 87 Vauxhall Walk, London SE11 5HJ • © 2018 Leslie Patricelli • The right of Leslie Patricelli to be
identified as the author and illustrator of this work has been asserted by her in accordance with the Copyright, Designs and Patents Act 1988
This book has been hand-lettered • Printed in China • All rights reserved. No part of this book may be reproduced, transmitted or stored in
an information retrieval system in any form or by any means, graphic, electronic or mechanical, including photocopying, taping and recording,
without prior written permission from the publisher. • British Library Cataloguing in Publication Data: a catalogue record for this book is
available from the British Library • ISBN 978-1-4063-8045-3 • www.walker.co.uk • 10 9 8 7 6 5 4 3 2 1

Bigger! Bigger!

Leslie Patricelli

WALKER BOOKS
AND SUBSIDIARIES
LONDON · BOSTON · SYDNEY · AUCKLAND

Build.

Bigger! Bigger!

Stronger!

Stronger!